A
Wild Goose Chase

A Wild Goose Chase

by Roy Toothaker

Illustrated by Tom Dunnington

Prentice-Hall, Inc., Englewood Cliffs, N.J.

Printed in the United States of
America · J

Prentice-Hall International, Inc.,
London
Prentice-Hall of Australia, Pty. Ltd.,
North Sydney
Prentice-Hall of Canada, Ltd., Toronto
Prentice-Hall of India Private Ltd., New
Delhi
Prentice-Hall of Japan, Inc., Tokyo

Library of Congress Cataloging in
Publication Data

Toothaker, Roy.
    A wild goose chase.

    SUMMARY: Animals romp through
the woods, chasing and catching each
other.
    [1. Play—Fiction] I. Dunnington,
Tom.
II. Title.
PZ7.T64308Wi   [E]   75-11753
ISBN 0-13-959510-4

To *I. L. R.*

Out of the meadow,

and over the log where I was hiding,

a goose chased a frog,

chasing a chicken,

chasing a hog,

chasing a chipmunk,

chasing a dog,

chasing a polliwog,

chasing a chinch bug,
searching for oats in a bog.

The goose caught the frog,

who caught the chick,

who caught the hog,

who caught the 'munk,

who caught the dog,

who caught the 'wog,

who caught the bug, searching for oats in a bog.

And I caught the goose!